This book belongs to

. . . .

Fun Ideas for the Storyteller

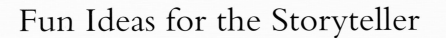

Nigel's Numberless World is an entertaining story about numbers and counting. Many children will identify with Nigel's number problem, and come away reassured that numbers are useful and not too difficult after all!

Read on to find out how to get the most fun out of this story.

Read, count, and look

Read the story with expression! Let your child hear the growing confusion of Nigel's numberless world. She will want to join in with the *Whizz Bang*s of the magic watch. Encourage her to count along as you read – perhaps help Nigel count the goals he scores and the number of presents at his birthday party. When you get to the end of the story, look around and see how many numbers your child can find in her own world.

WHIZZ! BANG!!

What's in the bubble?

Children may not be sure about speech bubbles so remind your child that they contain the words the character is saying or thinking. Read the words in the bubbles together. Your child might also find clues in the artwork, such as word labels on objects, that can help tell the story. How many can you find?

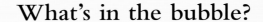

Useful numbers?

If your child is interested, talk about the ways that numbers are used in this book, such as for counting, measuring, and telling time. Ask her to count the eggs in the breakfast scene – would there be enough or too many for your family? Talk about brothers and sisters. How does Nigel feel about his brother? Nigel looks forward to his birthday. Look at a calendar to count how many days until your child's next birthday.

Picture your feelings

Look at the pictures carefully with your child. Pictures often tell us how people are feeling. How does Mum feel when she is trying to bake the cake? How does Nigel feel after the football game? What about when the numbers come back with a *Whizz Bang*?

Do as much counting as your child wants and enjoy the story!

Wendy Cooling
Reading Consultant

I like numbers!

To Richard, Tabitha and Archie
with lots of love. L.C.
To Mr Gilmore who made numbers make sense. N.L.

Dorling **DK** Kindersley

LONDON, NEW YORK, SYDNEY, DELHI, PARIS,
MUNICH and JOHANNESBURG

First published in Great Britain in 2000
by Dorling Kindersley Limited,
9 Henrietta Street, London WC2E 8PS

2 4 6 8 10 9 7 5 3 1

A CIP catalogue record for this book is available from the British Library.

ISBN 0-7513-7228-5

Colour reproduction by Dot Gradations, UK

Printed in Hong Kong by Wing King Tong

Acknowledgements:
Series Reading Consultant: Wendy Cooling   **Series Activities Advisor**: Lianna Hodson
Photographer: Steve Gorton   **Models**: Hannah Partridge, Ryan Heaton, Cherise and Chris Stephenson

For our complete
catalogue visit
www.dk.com

Nigel's Numberless World

Lucy Coats

Illustrated by Neal Layton

DK

A Dorling Kindersley Book

Nigel and Tom were brothers. Nigel was good at lots of things, but Tom was nearly *always* better. Tom was especially good at numbers.

Tom could count how many sweets to share out. Nigel couldn't.

Tom knew what time their favourite television programme started. Nigel didn't.

And Tom *always* beat him at number dominoes.

Worst of all, Tom knew exactly how many days it was to his birthday. Nigel only knew it was 'soon'. Nigel just couldn't be bothered with numbers.

One Saturday morning Nigel woke up early. He ran down to see if the postman had been. There on the mat was an early birthday present with a note that said:
To Nigel, If it's numbers you fear,
why not make them disappear?
Love, Uncle Ted.

He quickly ripped off the paper before Mum could stop him. Inside was a big blue watch with a red button on the side. Nigel pressed the button.
Suddenly, all the numbers on the watch face disappeared.

When Nigel went into the kitchen, Mum had a big pan on the stove. She was cooking eggs. Lots and lots of eggs!

"Oh Nigel!" she wailed. "I don't know what's the matter with me. I just can't count anything this morning." Nigel ate as many eggs as he could, but there were still lots left over for Dad and Tom.

Outside, their neighbour Mr Jones was standing scratching his head. He was looking up and down the road as if he didn't know where he was. Nigel looked at the houses. There were no numbers on them!

At the corner shop, Nigel chose his favourite comic and took some coins out of his pocket to pay.

"Oh no, Nigel!" said Mrs Mackenzie, the shop owner. "These are no good. There are no numbers on them! Perhaps you could swap something instead."

Nigel turned out his pockets. There, in among the sticky sweet papers, was his favourite bouncing ball. He handed it over glumly.

Tom teased Nigel about his numberless money
all the way home.

Nigel opened the kitchen door and sniffed. He could smell something. "Perhaps Mum's making my birthday cake," he thought excitedly. But Mum was looking worried.

"There aren't any numbers in this recipe book! I'll have to guess," she said, tipping ingredients into a bowl. Nigel had a secret taste. Yuck! Too much sugar!

Mum looked at the oven. "Oh dear, where are the numbers on here?" she muttered, twiddling the knobs. Soon there was a horrid burning smell.

Nigel was worried. His birthday wouldn't be the same without a cake.

Later that afternoon, Dad took Nigel and Tom to the park for a game of football. Nigel was good at football, just as good as Tom.

"I'll keep score," said Dad.

Nigel tried really hard. He dodged and passed and kicked the ball and scored lots of goals, lots more than Tom he was sure. It was his best game ever.

But Dad couldn't seem to count up the goals, so nobody won. Nigel sulked. It was really unfair.

On the way home they stopped at the shoe shop. Nigel needed new trainers. "I'm not sure what size he is," said Dad.

"Hmm," said the assistant as he stared at Nigel's smelly feet. But he couldn't measure them and none of the shoes had any sizes on them anyway. Nigel groaned as he tried on one pair after another. They were all either too big or too small.

When they arrived home, Nigel went straight upstairs to his bedroom. He didn't like this numberless world. It was too confusing. And he was *starving* after playing football. Surely it must be time for tea now! He pressed the button on his talking robot alarm clock.

Nigel sighed. As he slowly started to count out his toy pirates for a battle, he thought about how really *useful* numbers were.

Just then, the door opened and Tom burst in.

"Yaharr! I am Tom the Terror of the Seas, and you are my prisoner!" yelled Tom, scattering pirates everywhere.

Nigel found himself on the floor with a heavy brother on his tummy. "Gerroff!" he groaned. "You're hurting me!"

But Tom was already rolling off. He had noticed Nigel's new watch.

Tom pressed the red button. WHIZZ! BANG!
Suddenly all the numbers were back.

Nigel peered at the numbers on the watch face. He thought hard – very hard. And the harder he thought, the more he began to understand.

"It's four o'clock," he said. "It's tea time!"

Then he looked at the calendar hanging on the wall. He counted on his fingers, and again on his toes to be sure.

And it was. At his birthday party, Nigel counted the FIVE candles flickering on his cake and the SIX presents from his friends waiting to be unwrapped.

But the best part of the day came when he beat Tom at number dominoes. Tom had better look out – Nigel the Number Genius was on his way!

Activities to Enjoy

If you've enjoyed this story, you might like to try some of these simple, fun activities with your child.

Play number rhymes

This lively activity is a good way to introduce your child to numbers. Start with a number that your child is familiar with, such as his/her age.

FIVE little ducks went out one day,
Over the hills and far away.
Mother Duck said,
Quack! Quack! Quack! Quack!
But only FOUR little ducks came back.

FOUR little ducks went out one day,
Over the hills and far away.
Mother Duck said,
Quack! Quack! Quack! Quack!
But only THREE little ducks came back.

THREE little ducks . . . but only TWO little ducks came back.

TWO little ducks . . . but only ONE little duck came back.

ONE little duck . . . but NONE of those little ducks came back.

Mother Duck, she went out one day
Over the hills and far away,
Mother Duck, she said,
Quack! Quack! Quack! Quack!
and ALL of those little ducks came back!

Other number rhymes to try:
One, Two, Buckle My Shoe; Ten Green Bottles; Five Little Speckled Frogs

Adding fun

Use objects to show addition and subtraction. It's much easier to understand when your child can see and count the numbers. Nigel has four presents. His friends give him two more presents. How many presents does he have all together?

Number dominoes

Help your child get used to numbers by playing games such as dominoes. You can easily make a set of twenty-eight domino cards out of paper. For younger children, use pictures or dots they can count. Older children will be able to play with written numerals from one to six. Each of two players gets eight cards. The first player lays down a domino. The next player tries to match one of his cards with the one on the table, for example, two dots with the number two. If he can't, he takes a spare card. The first player to use all their dominoes wins.

or

Make textured numbers

Write a number on a piece of paper with glue. Ask your child to stick on something such as glitter or pasta to make a textured number. Or make a number badge with your child's age. Cut a circle out of a piece of card and write "I am" on it. Your child can add a textured number for her age.

I AM 3   I AM 4   I AM 5   I AM 6

Other Share-a-Story titles to collect:

Not Now, Mrs Wolf!
by Shen Roddie
illustrated by Selina Young

The Caterpillar That Roared
by Michael Lawrence
illustrated by Alison Bartlett

Are You Spring?
by Caroline Pitcher
illustrated by Cliff Wright